The Case of the Golden Key

SCHOLASTIC
ACTION™

Welcome to This Book

Have you ever had something turn out differently than you expected?

When Jigsaw Jones first meets Reginald, he doesn't like him. Reginald has just moved into a fancy house and doesn't seem friendly. Jigsaw thinks he's just a rich snob. But then Reginald asks Jigsaw to help solve a mystery. He's found a golden key hidden in a box. And there's a note. Perhaps it will tell them what the key opens.

As Jigsaw tackles the case, what will he learn about the key? What will he find out about Reginald?

Target Words

These words will help you unlock the mystery of the golden key.

- **coincidence:** something that happens by chance
  Was it a coincidence that Reginald found the golden key—or did someone want him to find it?

- **observe:** to notice; to watch someone or something carefully
  Detectives observe things that most people don't.

- **obvious:** very easy to see or understand
  Jigsaw won't be able to solve this mystery by looking in the obvious places.

Reader Tips

Here's how to get the most out of this book.

- **Parts of a Book** Understanding the parts of a book can help you as you read. The table of contents lists the book's chapter titles. Chapter titles let you know what kind of information is in each chapter. What do you think Chapter 10 is about?

- **Character** Think about how Jigsaw and the other characters are described. Watch for what they think, say, and do.

The Case of the Golden Key

by James Preller

illustrated by Jamie Smith

cover illustration by R. W. Alley

SCHOLASTIC INC.

New York   Toronto   London   Auckland   Sydney
Mexico City   New Delhi   Hong Kong   Buenos Aires

For Max and Julia.

And another big assist to Maria Barbo,
for helping give this book its heart.
—JP

Text copyright © 2002 by James Preller.
Illustrations copyright © 2002 by Scholastic Inc.
All rights reserved. Published by Scholastic Inc.
Printed in the U.S.A.

ISBN 0-439-57941-4

1 2 3 4 5 6 7 8 9 10   23   12 11 10 09 08 07 06 05 04 03

Contents

Chapter One

Reginald Pinkerton Armitage III

Sunday morning I was riding uphill, on my way to meet a new client. His house was on the edge of town. But it might as well have been the edge of the world. A neighborhood of long driveways and fancy cars. The houses came in three sizes: big, bigger, and just plain ridiculous.

I arrived at 86 Baker Street, snapped down the kickstand, and took a look around. There was a lot of around to look at. The front lawn was so perfect it could have been the infield grass at Yankee Stadium.

The bushes looked like they'd been trimmed with a pair of small scissors and a tweezer. The house itself was a little bigger than just plain ridiculous.

I glanced down at my faded jeans and beat-up sneakers. I tucked in my shirt. Pulled down my hat. And did three quick push-ups on the doorbell.

Gong-gong-gong, it chimed.

The thick door opened without a sound.

 2

That was the first time I laid eyes on Reginald Pinkerton Armitage III. He was shorter than me, though he stood as straight as a U.S. Marine. Reginald was dressed in crisp khakis and a sweater vest over a button-down shirt. He wore a tidy bow tie and his slick black hair was held in place by gooey gel. With his right pinky, Reginald pushed a pair of round eyeglasses from the tip of his nose closer to his face.

He eyed me with all the warmth of a sick goldfish. "And you might be . . . ?"

"I *might* be Jigsaw Jones," I answered. "At least that's the name on the card."

I handed him my business card.

NEED A MYSTERY SOLVED?
Call Jigsaw Jones
or Mila Yeh!
for a dollar a day,
we make problems go away.

CALL 555–4523 or 555–4374

3

He glanced at the card, looked me over, and stepped aside. "Do come in."

So I did.

With a voice as formal as a tuxedo, he asked, "May I take your hat?"

"Take it where?"

That made him blink. "Off your head, naturally."

"The hat goes where I go," I replied. "It's a package deal."

He frowned. "Your shoes are filthy. Place them on the mat by the door."

I didn't make a move. Instead, we stood staring at each other like two cowboys in a showdown. Meanwhile, silence rolled by like a tumbleweed.

"I meant to say, *would* you place your shoes on the mat . . . *please*?" Reginald blurted.

"Say 'pretty please,' put a cherry on top, and I'll think about it," I replied.

Chapter Two

Truce

Reginald's face flushed a deep red. "I don't care for your tone," he scolded.

I replied with a long, slow yawn. *Ho-hum*.

Reginald brushed past me, yanked open the door, and scowled. "Please leave now," he demanded.

"Loosen up, Reggie," I replied. "We're just getting to know each other."

"That's *Reginald*," he snapped. "And I don't care for your lack of manners."

"*My* manners?" I gasped. "Tell you what, let's start over. Only this time, maybe you

try to work up a smile. You called me, remember?"

Reginald's eyes widened in shock. He wasn't used to getting his toes stepped on. He stammered, "I . . . I daresay . . . yes, perhaps . . . quite right, quite right."

He pulled off his glasses, fumbled with them for a few seconds, then placed them back on his nose. "Perhaps we've gotten off to a bad start." He thrust out a hand. "My name is Reginald Pinkerton Armitage III. But if you must, you may call me . . . Reggie."

A weak smile drifted across his face.

I took his hand and shook it. "Jones," I said. "Jigsaw Jones. Private eye."

Reginald gestured down the long hallway. "Shall we . . . er . . ." He glanced once again at my feet. "I'm awfully sorry, but it's a house rule."

Well, my sneakers *were* muddy. Stepping on the heel, I slipped out of one sneaker,

then the other. I was glad to see my socks matched. Too bad my right big toe poked through like a beached white whale.

Again, Reginald's lips headed south in a frown.

"Would you care for a pair of slippers?" he offered.

"No, thanks," I replied. "Never on Sundays."

"I see you're a wiseguy," he observed.

"Only when I need to be," I replied. "Look, Reginald Pinkerton Armitage III. You told me on the phone that it was an emergency. I dropped everything, hopped on my bike, and rode all the way out here. Up three big hills, against the wind." I paused, a little weary. "You got any grape juice?"

"Grape juice?"

"How about just a few grapes?" I suggested. "I'll stomp on 'em myself."

This time, Reginald smiled. A real, honest-to-goodness smile. "All right, then. I'll instruct Madge to prepare refreshments. You're funny, Jones. I am beginning to like you."

"I'm beginning to like myself, too," I mumbled. "Lead the way, Reginald. I'll tag along behind."

Reginald started down the hallway. "We'll sit in the library," he informed me. "We can talk about the case in private there."

Reginald brought me to a large paneled

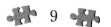

room, then left to "inquire" about refreshments. It was the kind of room you see in old black-and-white movies — before you switch the channel to Nickelodeon. Tall bookcases rose to the ceiling. A large desk filled one corner of the room. A few high-backed armchairs were placed here, there, and everywhere. Fancy reading lamps sat beside each one. A dusty gray cat lay snoozing on the rug, warmed by slanting rays of sunlight. A lazy ceiling fan pushed the air around.

Reginald returned, carrying a silver tray. "Milk and cucumber sandwiches," he announced.

"Oh, joy," I grumbled.

Reginald sat across from me. "I'd like to begin by asking you a few questions."

"Shoot."

He glanced at my business card. "Where is your partner, Mila Yeh?"

"She's tickling the ivories," I answered.

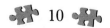 10

Reginald raised an eyebrow.

"A piano lesson," I explained. "I'll give her the facts later."

"It's just you and me, then," Reginald replied. "How splendid."

"Yeah, ain't it nice," I cooed. I eyed the tray of cucumber sandwiches and decided against it.

It wasn't a hard call to make.

I was hungry. But I wasn't *that* hungry.

Chapter Three
The Golden Key

I spent the next five minutes telling Reginald about detective work.

"Can you be trusted to keep a secret?" he asked me.

"Trusted? That's up to you," I said. "But since you're asking, yes. I can be trusted."

Reggie crossed the room to the desk. The dusty cat watched him with mild interest, one eye open. Reginald opened a drawer and lifted out a small box. He handed it to me. There was a sheet of paper on top with a neatly written list of birthdays.

KEY BIRTHDAYS

January 5	Evelyn
January 20	Cynthia
March 9	Imogene
April 3	Jules
April 9	Ada
June 1	Frederick
June 14	Basil
October 20	Gus
November 8	Douglas
November 31	Topper
December 20	Harold

I placed the sheet on the end table beside me. Inside the box, there was a bundle of red satin cloth.

"Look inside," Reginald instructed.

I unwrapped the cloth. It contained an old-fashioned skeleton key, about the length of a finger. Though not large, it was unusually heavy. I wondered if it was solid gold.

"What does it open?" I asked.

"That's what I'd like you to find out," Reginald said. "And I'm prepared to pay for it."

"I get a dollar a day, plus expenses."

"Money is not a problem," he promised.

"Speak for yourself," I countered.

Reginald pulled a money clip from his shirt pocket. It was stuffed with crisp green bills. He peeled off a ten spot and handed it

to me. "Alexander Hamilton," I noted. "An all-around swell guy."

I stuffed the ten-dollar bill into my pocket. Taking out a black marker, I scribbled in my detective journal:

CLIENT: Reginald Pinkerton Armitage III
CASE: The Golden Key

"Where did you find the box?" I asked.

Reginald reached for a cucumber sandwich. He ate slowly with his pinky extended, careful not to drop crumbs.

"This old house used to be owned by my great-uncle, Simon Rathgate, Esquire," he said. "Great-uncle Rathgate made his fortune in stocks and bonds. Millions upon millions of dollars. He passed away two years ago. The house has been empty ever since."

"Until you moved in," I noted.

"Yes, this past summer." Reginald

nodded. "His things were left here — the furniture, the paintings, and so on. The house, too, is quite interesting. Though I've lived in better, naturally."

"Naturally," I echoed.

"Father is an international banker. We move around a lot. Switzerland, London, San Francisco, that kind of thing. Now we're here, of all places."

"You don't like it here?" I asked.

Reginald's lips tightened. "No, not much. I'm schooled at home by tutors, and I don't have many friends." He gave a forced laugh. "The truth is, Jones, I don't have *any* friends. Just my sister, Hildegard."

"Well, she's your friend, isn't she?" I said.

"Sisters don't count," Reginald stated. He fell silent, chewing sadly on a sorry excuse for a sandwich.

"What about the box?" I prodded.

"This old house, you see, has many

strange features. False doors, secret rooms, that sort of thing. Hildegard and I found the box while we were searching through Great-uncle Rathgate's old bedroom. The box was tucked far back on a top shelf. It's only by pure luck that we found it."

"You tried the key in all the obvious places," I said.

"Oh, yes. I've looked all over the house. It doesn't fit anything."

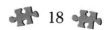

I weighed the key in my hand. "Don't get your hopes up," I cautioned him. "The world is full of lost keys without locks."

Reginald leaned forward, suddenly earnest. "I'm *sure* that key opens something special. Why else would it have been tucked away in a box? And," he added, "I can already tell that you're the one who'll help me find the treasure."

"Treasure?"

"I mean, um, find the solution. I have no idea what the key opens, naturally," Reginald declared.

"Naturally," I repeated. I'd heard enough. I wrapped the key in the cloth and placed it back in the box. I paused, studying the list. "That's odd," I murmured.

"Odd?" Reginald asked.

"It's a list of birthdays," I said.

"Yes, it seems so."

I handed it to Reginald. "Look at Topper's birthday. November thirty-first."

 19

Reginald shook his head. "I'm sorry, but I fail to understand."

"There *is no* November thirty-first," I said. "Don't you remember the poem? Thirty days hath September, April, June, and November."

"I see," Reginald answered. "But what does it mean?"

"It means that this may not be a list of birthdays after all," I said. "It's probably a secret code."

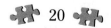

Chapter Four

The Hat Project

I didn't get to tell Mila about the case until Monday morning. We met at the bus stop.

"Who is this kid anyway?" Mila asked. "Reginald Pinkthumb . . . Arm-a-whoosie?"

"Reginald Pinkerton Armitage III," I corrected. "I don't know much about him. He's new in town. He told me he doesn't have any friends. To be honest, I could see why."

"You didn't like him?" Mila asked.

"I liked him, I guess," I said with a shrug.

"It's hard to explain. He was more like a grown-up than a kid."

"Oh, that's too bad," Mila stated. "Did you bring the key with you?"

"Nope, it's safe at home," I explained. "I brought the birthday list, though. I think it's written in code, but I'm not getting anywhere with it."

Mila folded the list neatly, then zipped it

in her backpack. "Don't worry, Jigsaw. We'll put our heads together at lunch."

Monday was a big day in room 201. After the usual morning routine, Ms. Gleason made an announcement. "This week, all of grade two will be working on the Hat Project." She gave Athena Lorenzo a stack of papers to hand out. "Please take these papers home to your parents."

She continued, "I'll assign a different hat to each of you. You'll do research at the library and at home — use dictionaries, encyclopedias, nonfiction books, even the Internet if you'd like. Then you'll make a poster with a drawing of your hat, including interesting facts."

"Interesting facts . . . about a hat?" Ralphie Jordan wondered.

Ms. Gleason smiled. "These hats are from all over the world, Ralphie. They are worn by people from different cultures

and for very different reasons. I'm sure you'll enjoy the research once you get into it."

Then came the moment of truth. As we all sat, excited and nervous, Ms. Gleason walked around the room. She placed a slip of paper on each of our desks.

"All right!" Bigs Maloney hooted. "I've got the bearskin hat!"

"What does a bearskin hat look like?" Danika Starling asked.

Bigs shrugged. "Beats me, but it sounds cool."

Joey Pignattano got the stovepipe hat. Lucy Hiller got the *chullo*, and Helen Zuckerman got the deerstalker.

Please, I thought, *please let me get the baseball cap.*

Kim Lewis got the slouch hat, Geetha Nair got the beret, and Bobby Solofsky got the gaucho hat, which was fine by me.

Then it was Mila's turn. "The dunce cap?!" she exclaimed. "Hey, what's the big idea, Ms. Gleason?"

"Oh, Mila, please. It's nothing personal. I think the history behind the dunce cap is fascinating. You'll enjoy it, believe me."

Mila slumped in her chair, glowering.

Ms. Gleason paused in front of my desk. She picked one slip, then changed her mind. She placed a different slip facedown on my desk. I turned it over: THE BASEBALL CAP!

I smiled at Ms. Gleason. She gave me a sly wink.

"Ms. Gleason," I said. "You rock."

"Yes," she answered. "And I roll, too."

Chapter Five
Busting the Code

Mila and I devoured our lunches in a hurry. Then we placed the list on the table.

Mila studied the page in silence, pulling on her long black hair. "Hmmm," she said. "It says, 'Key Birthdays.' Do you think that's a clue?"

"Good thinking," I agreed. "*Key* birthdays — like maybe the golden key."

Mila nodded. "It was good you pointed out November thirty-first. I would not have noticed that."

"What about the names?" I asked. "Don't they seem strange to you?"

Mila read a few of them out loud: "Imogene, Jules, Ada, Topper, Basil. I don't know, they sound British to me. Let's try naming some codes we already know."

I ticked off a bunch on my fingers . . . until I ran out of fingers. "There's the color code, the telephone code, the space code, the crease code, the vowel code, the substitution code. . . ."

"Okay, okay," Mila interrupted. "Sorry I asked. We're going to have to take this one code at a time. Let's start with the simplest of all, the substitution code."

In my journal, I jotted down the numbers one through twenty-six. Next to each number, starting with one, I wrote the letters A through Z. This way 1 = **A**, 2 = **B**, 3 = **C**, right on to 26 = **Z**.

"January *fifth*," I said. "That would be the letter *E*."

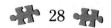

"What about the month?" Mila asked. "Do you think it means anything?"

"A mystery is like a jigsaw puzzle," I said. "You can only solve it . . ."

". . . one piece at a time," Mila added, finishing my sentence. She'd heard me say it a dozen times before.

"January *twentieth* would be *T*."

"March *ninth* is *I*."

"April *third* is *C*."

We continued down the list, skipping November thirty-first because there weren't that many letters in the alphabet.

"What does it spell?" Mila asked.

"ETICIANTHT!"

Yeesh.

Back to the drawing board.

"Hey, Jigsaw. I just noticed something," Mila pointed out. "This list is in order by month."

"So?"

"So maybe you were right. There *is*

something funny about these names: Ada, Basil, Cynthia, Douglas, Evelyn . . ."

Suddenly, I understood. A, B, C, D, E!

Mila scribbled down the list on a fresh sheet of paper. But this time, she listed the names in alphabetical order. Now it looked like this:

April 9	Ada
June 14	Basil
January 20	Cynthia
November 8	Douglas
January 5	Evelyn
June 1	Frederick
October 20	Gus
December 20	Harold
March 9	Imogene
April 3	Jules
November 31	Topper

"Now try the substitution code again," Mila insisted.

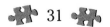

I did. "Now it spells I-N-T-H-E-A-T-T-I-C."

"Oh, my gosh," Mila nearly screamed. "IN . . . THE . . . ATTIC!"

"Great work, Mila!" I exclaimed. "You're brilliant!"

"Maybe," Mila said with a sigh. "But then how come Ms. Gleason gave me the dunce cap?"

Chapter Six
Hildy

A girl's voice answered the phone. "Hello, Armitage residence."

"Is Reginald home? This is Jigsaw."

"Oh, the famous detective!" she squealed. "Are you calling about the golden key?"

"Maybe," I answered. "Is this Hildegard?"

"Call me Hildy," she replied cheerily. "Only my parents and little brother call me Hildegard. What an awful name!"

I couldn't argue with that. "I suppose Reginald told you about me."

She chuckled softly. "Actually, I was the one who told Reginald to call you."

"How did you know about my detective business?" I wondered. "It's not like I run commercials on the radio."

"My friend Shirley Hitchcock mentioned your name," she replied. "Or maybe it was Barney Fodstock. Or Ben Ewing. To be honest, I've met so many people lately it's hard to remember who said what."

"Sounds like you've got a lot of friends," I said. "Reginald claims he hasn't met anyone."

Hildy was quiet for a moment. "I guess I'm the social butterfly in the family," she confessed. "Reginald keeps to himself. It isn't easy for him to meet new people."

"Yeah, I've met ice cubes that were warmer," I said.

"But you don't *know* Reginald!" she protested. "He's a great kid. It takes Reginald

a little while to feel comfortable. You could become friends, Jigsaw. You never know."

"I suppose," I replied. "Anyway, is Mr. Armitage III home or ain't he?"

Hildy left to find her brother. A few moments later, Reginald came to the phone.

I told him about the secret message. "Have you looked in the attic?" I asked.

"I wouldn't dare step foot up there!" he exclaimed.

"Why not?"

"My parents strictly forbid it."

"Reggie, Reggie, Reggie," I murmured. "Your parents forbid *you*. Did they say anything about me?"

"Of course not!" Reginald responded. "They've never even met —"

"So it's settled, then," I interrupted. "When can Mila and I come over?"

Reginald's voice changed. "There's another problem."

"There usually is," I replied.

Reginald explained, "I believe there's something spooky living in the attic. I've heard strange cries, and scratching and clawing sounds."

"That's why I get paid the big bucks," I said. "Just show us where the attic is. We'll handle the boogey monster."

After some hesitation, Reginald gave in. "Oh, all right," he said. "Tomorrow night, after supper. My parents won't be home."

Chapter Seven
In the Attic

Mila showed up at my door on Tuesday night — wearing a dunce cap. "Where'd you get that thing?" I asked.

"I made it last night," Mila said. "It's a dunce cap."

"I know it's a dunce cap," I replied. "But why are you wearing it?"

Mila smiled. "Ms. Gleason was right. Dunce caps really are cool."

She told me all about it. "There was this guy, John Duns Scotus. He lived a real long time ago. And he had all these crazy

ideas. He thought that if people wore these cone-shaped hats it would improve their learning. He thought the shape of the cone would help their heads absorb more information."

"That's nuts," I observed.

Mila said that a lot of other people thought so, too. They figured that John Duns Scotus's ideas were silly and called all his followers dunces. The nickname stuck.

After a while, teachers began to make kids wear dunce caps to punish them.

My brother Billy strolled into the room, jingling a set of car keys. "You ready, Worm? Let's hit the road." Billy was happy to give us a ride to Reginald's house. He borrowed my mom's car any chance he got.

Ten minutes later, Billy eased the car up Reginald's long driveway. He whistled. "Yowsa, this is some fancy chicken coop."

"Yeah, Jigsaw," Mila agreed. "You said it was big. But this house is . . ."

"Just plain ridiculous," I chimed in. "We'll be done in about an hour," I told Billy. "You can pick us up then."

"Sure thing, detective," Billy answered.

Reginald met us at the door, wearing a smile. It looked good on him. Once again, I slipped off my shoes in the hallway. But this time, I wore new socks.

Reginald led us up one flight of stairs,

then another. He pulled a string that hung from the hallway ceiling. It was an attic hatchway. A folding ladder dropped down. Above, it was as dark as night.

Strange noises came from the darkness. Mila looked at me with alarm.

I gritted my teeth and climbed a few steps. "I'll go first. Ready?"

Mila handed a flashlight up to me and followed.

"I'll wait here," Reginald volunteered.

The attic was a huge cluttered room filled with dark shapes. Mila sneezed. "Yuck, it's so dusty up here," she complained.

"I guess the maid doesn't make it up here too often," I cracked.

Mila sneezed — twice — in reply.

"Jigsaw, point that flashlight over here," she said. "I think there's a light."

Mila pulled on a string that lit a flickering, bare bulb that dangled from a cord. Now

shadows swayed around us, falling across our faces. The attic, with so many turns and dark corners, remained mostly in the dark.

"Let's get this over with," I urged. "The faster we're done, the faster we're out of here."

There was a jumble of old furniture stacked against a wall. Piles of boxes, old rugs, and other junk were scattered everywhere. We tried the key in one old desk, then in a dresser. Nothing worked.

"What's that?" Mila asked, pointing toward the back of the attic.

There was a black shape, about two feet in height, crouching in the corner. I walked slowly toward it. I took a deep breath and felt it with my hand. "Just a tarp," I said with relief. I lifted the tarp and scanned the area with the flashlight. The attic floor was covered with a thick layer of dust. The tarp concealed an old trunk that had been there for years. "I'll try the key," I whispered.

The skeleton key slid smoothly into the lock. I gave it a turn. *Click.*

Suddenly, I felt a cold hand on the back of my neck. It was Mila. "Shhh," she hissed. "Listen."

Scritch, scritch . . . yooooowwwww.

Mila's hand tightened on my shoulder. "What's that?" she asked. Her voice was barely above a whisper.

I turned my head to follow the sound into the far corner of the attic.

Two red eyes stared back at me.

Floating in the darkness.

Roaaa-roooow, it cried again.

Chapter Eight

A Secret Staircase

I aimed the flashlight at the floating eyes.

"Ha!" Mila laughed nervously. "Just a cat. I wonder how she got up here?"

"Never mind the cat," I complained. "Let's see what's inside this trunk."

It didn't take us long to find the treasure. Because there was no treasure to find. Just old clothes, a tuxedo wrapped in plastic, a goofy-looking top hat, blankets, scarves, and a woolen overcoat. "Let's drag this back to the hatch," I said.

We hauled the heavy chest across the floor.

"Jones?" Reginald called up. "What's that awful noise? Did you find anything?"

I poked my head through the hatch. "Yeah, we found your cat. And we solved the mystery, too. Only it wasn't worth solving in the first place."

Reginald climbed to the top of the ladder.

He looked through the trunk, sighed, and snapped it shut. "It was nothing after all," he said. "All that trouble for nothing."

That's the way it goes with some cases. You win some, you lose some. "Let's go home," I said to Mila.

She didn't answer. I turned to look back.

But Mila was gone.

"Heeeeeere, kitty, kitty," Mila called from across the attic. "Psssst, psssst. Heeeeeere, kitty, kitty."

Then there was silence.

Suddenly, Mila's voice threaded through the gloom. "Jigsaw, Reginald! Come quick. You've got to see this!"

When we got to the spot where Mila was standing, well, she wasn't. Suddenly — "BOO!" — her head popped out from behind a small hidden doorway.

"It's a secret tunnel!" Mila exclaimed. "I was trying to find the cat. I saw her go into this little hole. I felt around and realized it

was a small door. Come on, let's see where it leads."

We crawled through the tight, cramped tunnel. Then it suddenly opened up to a space where we could stand. To our left was a staircase leading down. *Creak, moan, creak, groan.* The old wooden stairs complained with each step. Down, down, down we walked, with only the beam of the flashlight piercing the darkness.

After a long time, Mila suddenly stopped.

"Dead end," she announced. "There's only a little hole for the cat to crawl through. This must be how she gets up to the attic."

"Hold on," Reginald said. "Help me push."

Together, we leaned against the wall — and it suddenly fell open. *Crash!* We sprawled to the floor.

I stood up and bonked my head. Rattling noises followed. "It's a clothes closet," I said. We slid open the door and there we stood: in Hildy's bedroom!

Chapter Nine
Topper

Friday morning at school, everyone brought in their hat posters. We also brought in our hats, either real ones or hats we made at home. Bobby Solofsky came into room 201 hootin' and hollerin', "Yee-haw, git along, little dogies!"

"Hey, Solofsky. What are you supposed to be?" Bigs Maloney asked.

"I'm a rootin', tootin', South American cowboy!" Bobby shouted. "This here's my gaucho hat."

Oh, brother.

Lucy explained that her hat, the *chullo*, was a folk hat from the Andes. "It keeps my ears nice and toasty," she said, "though it does nothing for my hair. People who live high in the Andes Mountains knit these colorful hats to stay warm."

Geetha looked amazing in her beret. Sort of like a movie star. Then Joey walked in, wearing a cardboard stovepipe hat . . . and a fake beard!

He scratched his face unhappily. "Man, this thing itches," he griped.

"Why are you wearing a beard?" Helen asked.

"Don't you recognize me?" Joey asked. "I'm Abraham Lincoln. He wore a hat just like this. In fact, that's where he kept his most important papers."

"You look like the Cat in the Hat to me," quipped Ralphie.

"Well, he wore one, too," Joey answered.
"It's also called a chimney top or a top hat."

Ms. Gleason was thrilled with our posters.
She had us take turns telling the class about
our hats. I said that in the old days, before
they used gloves, outfielders used to catch
baseballs with their hats. I held up my
poster and continued, "The first complete

baseball uniforms were worn in 1869, by the first-ever professional team, the Cincinnati Red Stockings."

I liked Helen's deerstalker. It made her look like Sherlock Holmes. She said that hunters in Great Britain used to wear them all the time. "Deerstalkers are really warm," Helen told us. "And if it rains, the water rolls right off the brim!" To prove it, Helen suddenly dumped a cup of water on her head. She was right. The water slid right off onto the floor.

I enjoyed it so much, I wanted to see it again. So I drew a quick picture in my journal.

Ms. Gleason hung up our posters in the hall. Then we had to parade through a bunch of classrooms. Wearing a dunce cap was a little embarrassing for Mila. But I didn't mind. After all, I looked exactly like myself!

During the parade I noticed Mila pulling on her long black hair, mumbling to herself. I'd seen that look before. It meant her Thinking Machine was working.

"What are you thinking, Mila?" I asked.

Mila gestured toward Joey. "I've seen that hat somewhere before," she said.

"Yeah, on Abraham Lincoln's head," I replied.

"No, no, that's not it. I remember now,"

Mila exclaimed, snapping her fingers. "In Reginald's attic!"

Mila was right. It was exactly like one of the hats in the trunk. "Stovepipe, chimney top, top hat," she thought aloud. "*Topper* — that was a name on the birthday list, wasn't it?"

"Yeah, the one with the fake birthday," I replied.

"This may be crazy, Jigsaw," Mila said with growing excitement. "But we have to go back to Reginald's attic. I think we may have missed something."

Chapter Ten

The Pieces Come Together

We raced our bikes to Reginald's house after school. On the way, Mila sang:

"Who's afraid of the big bad attic,
the big bad attic, the big bad attic?
Who's afraid of the big bad attic?
Not Jigsaw or me!"

Typical Mila. Always changing the words around. Happily, she sang better than the Three Little Pigs.

Yeesh.

Hildy and Reginald were waiting at the front door. We explained everything. "There was a top hat in the old trunk," Mila said. "If you remember, Topper was a name on the birthday list. The name with the fake birthday. I think it's another clue, telling us where to look."

Reginald pushed his glasses back with his right pinky. "Are you suggesting that Great-uncle Rathgate wanted us to find a hat?"

"Not the hat," I corrected. "But what may be hidden *inside* the hat."

"Oh, like Abraham Lincoln," Hildy gushed. "He used to hide papers in his hat."

I eyed her suspiciously.

Hildy added with a shrug, "It was in a biography I read the other day."

"Can we borrow your flashlight?" Mila asked Reginald.

We followed Reginald into the kitchen. He poked around in a cabinet for a while, moving things around and muttering to

himself. "That's strange," Reginald stated. "The flashlight is always right here in case the lights go out. Mother's very strict about that."

"I know where it is," I spoke up. "I saw a flashlight in Hildy's bedroom the other night. It was on your dresser."

"Oh? Um, yes, you're right," Hildy admitted. "I was . . . um . . . fooling around with it the other day."

I didn't say what I was thinking.

But I was thinking plenty.

Back in the attic, the trunk was right where we'd left it. While Mila, Hildy, and Reginald looked inside, I wandered over to where the trunk used to be. "Jigsaw, don't you want to see?" Mila called after me.

"In a second," I said. "First I want to check something."

It was just as I'd thought. There was a neat rectangle where the trunk used to be. The floor was smooth and clean — without a speck of dust. Yet all around the outline of the trunk, there was a thick layer of dust. Even though a tarp had loosely covered the area around the trunk for years and years.

Supposedly.

Now all the pieces were coming together.

A picture was forming.

Just then, Reginald let out a shout. "I can't believe my eyes!" he yelped. "It's a miracle!"

Chapter Eleven
A Real Friend

"I've been looking for this for months!" he exclaimed.

"What is it?" Mila asked.

"A postage stamp," Reginald said, his voice brimming with excitement. "A very rare, very hard-to-find postage stamp. It was tucked inside the hat, just like you said, Jigsaw."

I watched him, scratching my head.

Reginald must have noticed the expression on my face. "I've got quite a magnificent stamp collection," he offered.

"You see, I'm a philatelist — a person who collects postage stamps." He held the stamp tenderly in his fingertips. "It appears to be in excellent condition."

"Why is one lousy stamp a big deal?" I wondered.

"It was printed in a series," Reginald told us. "I had every one, except for this. It hasn't been easy to track down."

Reginald kept on shaking his head in wonder. "It's simply astonishing to find it here," he declared. "How could Great-uncle Rathgate have known? What an amazing, amazing coincidence. Isn't it, Hildy?"

Hildy nodded happily, glad to see the smile bursting across her brother's face. It was true. All the coldness and crusty manners had vanished. Reginald Pinkerton Armitage III was like a new person. Laughing, smiling, bouncing on the tips of his toes.

Mila sneezed. "Let's get out of this dusty attic," she complained.

I made sure to be the last one to leave. When no one was looking, I tossed my hat on the attic floor, then shut the hatch behind me.

Downstairs, I clapped my hands together. "Well, that wraps up this case," I said.

Reginald thanked us a dozen times. "You have no idea what this stamp means to me," he claimed. "Jones, you've made me so happy."

I scratched my hair. "Oh, rats! My hat!" I groaned. "I must have dropped it in the attic. Reginald, would you mind getting it for me?"

"Sure thing, Jones!" Reginald stated. "It's the least I could do."

With Reginald gone, I turned to Hildy. "I won't tell him," I said. "But your Great-uncle Rathgate didn't have anything to do with that stamp. I know you're the one behind this."

Hildy denied it at first, but I waved her

 67

protests away. "You were there when Reginald found the key," I said. "I'm guessing that it wasn't an accident — because you placed it there."

Hildy grinned slightly.

"And it was your idea to hire me," I continued. "Then there was the secret staircase that led from your closet into the attic. I bet you've known about it for a

while. The flashlight in your room gave that away.

Hildy didn't bother denying it.

"Then there was the tarp that covered the chest," I added. "If it had been there for years, there wouldn't have been any dust under it. But there was. That means you put the tarp on recently, probably just to make the mystery more difficult."

"More *fun*," Hildy corrected. "I made it more fun — for Reginald and for you."

"True," I agreed.

"And the stamp," Mila added. "Only you could have known which stamp would have made Reginald so happy."

Hildy gave a sly grin. "He is happy, isn't he?"

She glanced toward the stairs. We heard footsteps coming closer. "He's been so lonely since we moved here," she confided. "I worry about my little brother. Me? I don't have trouble making friends. But it's hard on Reginald. He's like a grown-up trapped in a boy's body. Most kids don't understand him."

Mila smiled. "So you wanted to help him make new friends. Wow, what a great sister."

"What a great *friend*," I remarked.

"Here's your hat, Jones!" Reginald shouted, tossing it across the room.

"Nice throw," I commented, catching the hat with one hand.

My brother pulled up in the car. He tooted the horn softly. We turned to leave.

I stopped at the doorway. "Say, Reggie. You play ball?"

Reginald frowned. "I'm afraid I'm not very good."

"That's okay, neither am I," I lied. "Maybe I'll call you sometime. We could get a few kids together for a game. What do you say?"

Reginald blinked a few times. He smiled again. "I'd love to play baseball. Thanks."

We left, with Hildy and Reginald waving to us from the front door. I saw that Hildy's arm was wrapped around her brother's shoulder. She hugged him tightly.

"He's not so bad after all," I said to Mila. "I mean, once you get to know him."

Mila agreed. "Who knows? Maybe he'll make a few friends at the ballgame."

"I hope so," I said. "But no matter what, he's already got one true friend: his sister, Hildy. That's a pretty good start."

"Yes." Mila nodded. "One true friend."

My brother tooted the car horn again.

"Let's go, partner," I said.

"Sure, partner. Let's go."

Glossary

astonishing *(adjective)* surprising (p. 66)

brilliant *(adjective)* very smart (p. 32)

brim *(noun)* the wide part that sticks out around the bottom of a hat (p. 56)

client *(noun)* someone who uses the services of someone else (p. 1)

coincidence *(noun)* something that happens by chance (p. 66)

conceal *(verb)* to hide (p. 43)

counter *(verb)* to oppose (p. 15)

devour *(verb)* to eat quickly (p. 27)

earnest *(adjective)* very serious and interested (p. 19)

flush *(verb)* to blush, or turn red (p. 6)

forbid *(verb)* to order someone not to do something (p. 37)

gesture *(verb)* to move in a way that tells something (p. 7)

glower *(verb)* to stare angrily (p. 26)

inquire *(verb)* to ask for information (p. 10)

khakis *(noun)* tan cotton pants (p. 3)

observe *(verb)* to notice; to watch someone or something carefully (p. 8)

obvious *(adjective)* very easy to see or understand (p. 18)

prod *(verb)* to encourage, or push, someone to do something (p. 17)

quip *(verb)* to make a clever remark (p. 53)

research *(noun)* the study of a topic in order to learn more about it (p. 23)

ridiculous *(adjective)* silly or foolish (p. 1)

routine *(noun)* a regular way of doing something (p. 23)

scowl *(verb)* to frown angrily (p. 6)

tarp *(noun)* a large sheet of plastic or cloth used to cover something (p. 43)

tutor *(noun)* a teacher who gives private lessons to one student at a time (p. 17)

tuxedo *(noun)* a man's jacket, usually black, worn for special events (p. 5)

About the Author

James Preller often draws upon his own life as a basis for his Jigsaw Jones books. Like Jigsaw, James Preller has a slobbering, sock-eating dog. Like Jigsaw, James was the youngest in a large family. His older brothers called him Worm and worse — Yeesh! And so do Jigsaw's!

James and Jigsaw both love jigsaw puzzles, baseball, grape juice, and mysteries! But even though Jigsaw and James have so much in common, they are not the same person.

Unlike Jigsaw, James Preller is the author of more than 80 books for children, including *The Big Book of Picture-Book Authors & Illustrators; Wake Me in Spring, Hiccups for Elephant;* and *Cardinal & Sunflower.* He lives outside of Albany, New York in a town called Glenmont, with his wife, Lisa, three kids — Nicholas, Gavin, and Maggie — his cat, Blue, and his dog, Seamus.